SCIENTISTS AND THEIR DISCOVERIES

ALFRED NOBEL

KOHLER PUBLIC LIBRARY
KOHLER, WISCONSIN

SCIENTISTS AND THEIR DISCOVERIES

SCIENTISTS AND THEIR DISCOVERIES

ALFRED NOBEL

TIMMY WARNER

MASON CREST

Mason Crest
450 Parkway Drive, Suite D
Broomall, Pennsylvania 19008
(866) MCP-BOOK (toll-free)
www.masoncrest.com

Copyright © 2019 by Mason Crest, an imprint of National Highlights, Inc.

All rights reserved. No part of this publication may be reproduced or transmitted in any form or by any means, electronic or mechanical, including photocopying, recording, taping, or any information storage and retrieval system, without permission from the publisher.

Printed and bound in the United States of America.

CPSIA Compliance Information: Batch #SG2018.
For further information, contact Mason Crest at 1-866-MCP-Book.

First printing
9 8 7 6 5 4 3 2 1

Library of Congress Cataloging-in-Publication Data on file with the Library of Congress

ISBN: 978-1-4222-4026-7 (hc)
ISBN: 978-1-4222-7758-4 (ebook)

Scientists and their Discoveries series ISBN: 978-1-4222-4023-6

Developed and Produced by National Highlights Inc.
Interior and cover design: Yolanda Van Cooten
Production: Michelle Luke

QR CODES AND LINKS TO THIRD-PARTY CONTENT
You may gain access to certain third-party content ("Third-Party Sites") by scanning and using the QR Codes that appear in this publication (the "QR Codes"). We do not operate or control in any respect any information, products, or services on such Third-Party Sites linked to by us via the QR Codes included in this publication, and we assume no responsibility for any materials you may access using the QR Codes. Your use of the QR Codes may be subject to terms, limitations, or restrictions set forth in the applicable terms of use or otherwise established by the owners of the Third-Party Sites. Our linking to such Third-Party Sites via the QR Codes does not imply an endorsement or sponsorship of such Third-Party Sites or the information, products, or services offered on or through the Third-Party Sites, nor does it imply an endorsement or sponsorship of this publication by the owners of such Third-Party Sites.

Publisher's Note: Websites listed in this book were active at the time of publication. The publisher is not responsible for websites that have changed their address or discontinued operation since the date of publication. The publisher reviews and updates the websites each time the book is reprinted.

CONTENTS

KEY ICONS TO LOOK FOR:

Words to understand: These words with their easy-to-understand definitions will increase the reader's understanding of the text while building vocabulary skills.

Sidebars: This boxed material within the main text allows readers to build knowledge, gain insights, explore possibilities, and broaden their perspectives by weaving together additional information to provide realistic and holistic perspectives.

Educational videos: Readers can view videos by scanning our QR codes, providing them with additional educational content to supplement the text. Examples include news coverage, moments in history, speeches, iconic sports moments, and much more!

Text-dependent questions: These questions send the reader back to the text for more careful attention to the evidence presented there.

Research projects: Readers are pointed toward areas of further inquiry connected to each chapter. Suggestions are provided for projects that encourage deeper research and analysis.

Series glossary of key terms: This back-of-the-book glossary contains terminology used throughout the series. Words found here increase the reader's ability to read and comprehend higher-level books and articles in this field.

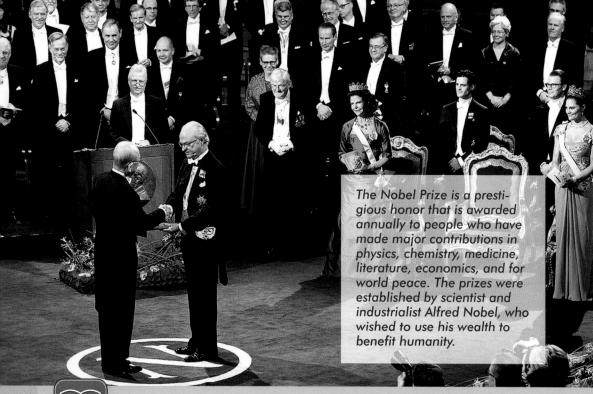

The Nobel Prize is a prestigious honor that is awarded annually to people who have made major contributions in physics, chemistry, medicine, literature, economics, and for world peace. The prizes were established by scientist and industrialist Alfred Nobel, who wished to use his wealth to benefit humanity.

WORDS TO UNDERSTAND

cellulose—an organic compound of carbon, hydrogen, and oxygen that forms the solid framework of plants. It is sometimes fibrous. If cotton and other forms of nearly pure cellulose are treated with nitric acid, a very highly explosive product, guncotton, is formed.

Greek Fire—a mixture of inflammable materials, the principal one probably being naphtha, used by the Byzantines in the defense of their empire.

high explosives—term usually used for the various nitro-compounds, as distinct from gunpowder.

naphtha—an inflammable hydrocarbon.

saltpeter—another name for potassium nitrate (KNO_3), a white crystalline salt used in the making of gunpowder.

sulfur—pale yellow, non-metallic element used in the making of gunpowder.

CHAPTER 1

Nobel and His Prizes

The annual award of Nobel Prizes is an event of worldwide interest. Apart from their actual value—running into many thousands of dollars—these awards are the highest possible recognition of achievement in science and medicine, in literature, and in the cause of peace. Among the past prizewinners—over 900 in all—are such famous people as Albert Einstein, Marie Curie, Martin Luther King, Barack Obama, and Malala Yousafzai. Over the years, the prizewinners have come from almost every country in the world; they receive their awards from the King of Sweden at an impressive ceremony in Stockholm.

The awards are made each year on the same day, December 10. The date is very significant, for it marks the anniversary of the death of an outstanding Swedish scientist, Alfred Nobel, whose remarkable industrial success made these prizes possible. Yet Nobel is less well known than many people who have received his prizes. There is a certain irony about this, for if the prizes had been founded by others in Nobel's lifetime, his own brilliance and success would probably have put him among the winners.

For this obscurity, Alfred Nobel himself was mainly responsible. Despite the scale of his worldwide industrial operations, he never courted publicity; indeed, he actively shunned it. To him, biography was of no interest. He did not trouble to put on record the sort of material that would help those who later sought to piece together the story of his life.

Pakistani activist Malala Yousafzai is the youngest person to win a Nobel Prize. She was just seventeen when she received the Nobel Peace Prize in 2014 for her work promoting education for children, especially young women, in poor countries.

Writing to his brother, he once said: "Who has time to read biographical accounts? And who can be so simple or so good-natured as to be interested in them?" Pressed further, he said: "No one reads essays except about actors and murderers."

Perhaps Nobel's desire for anonymity should have been respected. He is to most people a rather shadowy person, known more for the prizes he endowed than for his own achievements. But he should be more widely recognized as an outstanding scientist and industrialist, and his life was extremely interesting and colorful.

From this point of view, Nobel was a man of baffling contradictions.

Although he was immensely wealthy by the standards of his day, he lived relatively modestly and quietly. Generous to his guests, he was restrained with himself. Though his inventions greatly increased the destructiveness of military weapons, he was an ardent worker for the cause of peace. He received little formal education, yet he mastered many aspects of science and engineering, and became fluent in the principal European languages. At nineteen he was writing verse in English that would have done credit to some of the minor poets. Despite poor health, he was amazingly energetic; few people ever achieved more than he did. A shrewd industrialist, he well knew the vital importance of precisely worded legal contracts, yet he drafted his own all-important will so imprecisely that years of litigation were necessary before his wishes could be fulfilled.

To use a Latin tag, Alfred Nobel was a man *sui generis*: that is, one who fits no ordinary category. Before trying to unravel this complex web, we must, however, look at the main events in his life and the background against which they took place. As his main achievement was to build a vast international business to make **high explosives**, we have to first learn something of the history of this industry up to the time that Nobel began to take an interest in it.

The History of Explosives

The details of the discovery of gunpowder are still obscure, but the main facts are well known. From ancient times—certainly as early as 500 BCE—extensive military use was made of highly flammable materials. The most famous of these was the so called **Greek Fire** which, from the seventh century, played a big part in the defense of the Byzantine Empire. The exact composition of Greek Fire is unknown, and probably no standard recipe existed, but the main ingredient was **naphtha**.

In about the eleventh centur, the Chinese found that such mixtures burned even more fiercely if **saltpeter**—which yields oxygen on heating—was added to them. From this it was quite a short step to gunpowder— described, but not invented, by Roger Bacon in the thirteenth century—a

To learn more about Greek Fire, scan here:

mixture of saltpeter, charcoal, and **sulfur**. This is explosive in the sense that once ignited, it continues to burn even without air. A great quantity of hot gas is produced in a few seconds and the resulting high pressure can be used to bring about general destruction—for example, to destroy the foundations of a building—or controlled to fire projectiles from cannon or small arms such as muskets or pistols.

Artillery began to come into use in about the mid-thirteenth century, but Crécy (1346) was probably the first major European battle in which it was used. Guns were quite small at first, but as early as 1453, the Turks used a 19-ton cannon in the siege of Constantinople. At first solid balls were fired, of stone or iron. But quite soon hollow projectiles were filled with gunpowder, and fused to explode on reaching their target. Sometimes such explosive shells were filled with pieces of iron to rain a hail of small missiles on a massed enemy. Although explosive shells of this type were possibly used by the Venetians at Jadra in 1376, they were not widely used in warfare until the seventeenth century. Shrapnel, the invention of Henry Shrapnel (1761–1842), received official approval in 1803 and was extensively used in the Peninsular War and at Waterloo. The other important innovation in nineteenth-century artillery was that of the breech-loaded shell.

Meanwhile, hand firearms had begun to replace the long bow and the cross bow, which were old fashioned, though by no means extinct, by the seventeenth century. At first hand guns were clumsy, inaccurate weapons, laboriously loaded by the muzzle and fired by applying a flame to a touch-hole. But they evolved into accurate, reliable, quickfiring weapons. Spiral grooving of the barrel (rifling) gave a spin to the bullet, and greatly improved the accuracy. This device was known in the sixteenth century, for sporting purposes, but rifles did not come widely into military use until the Thirty Years' War (1618–48). The introduction of the percussion cap early in the nineteenth century provided a more reliable, weatherproof firing action.

The Ottoman Turks used enormous siege guns to capture the fortress at Constantinople in 1453, marking the end of the Byzantine Empire.

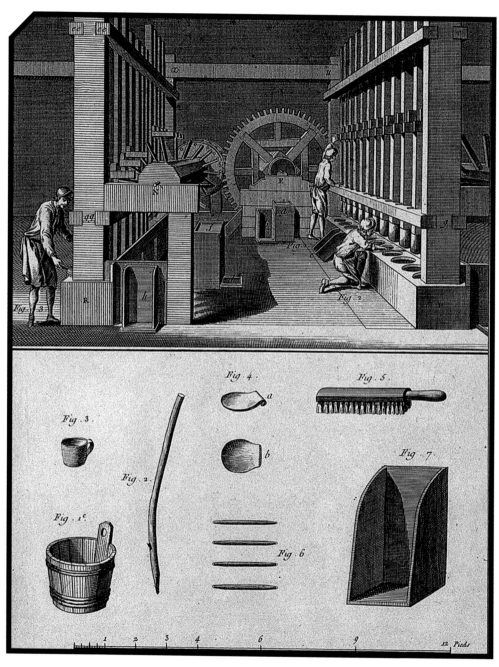

This eighteenth-century illustration from a French book shows a factory where gunpowder is manufactured, as well as the tools used to produce it.

Finally, there was the introduction of the breech-loading cartridge, replacing the cumbersome method of muzzle-loading with a ramrod.

From the early days of gunpowder, military engineers had used it for undermining enemy fortifications, and from the 1600s it was used for blasting in mines and quarries. These were hazardous operations, but the risk was much reduced by William Bickford's invention of the safety fuse in 1831.

Swedish reenactors fire an artillery piece during a reenactment of a battle from the Thirty Years' War. The gunpowder used in muskets and cannons produced thick smoke that obscured battlefields, as well as residue that could make the weapons less accurate.

Nineteenth-Century Improvements

By the mid-nineteenth century, the military and civil use of explosives was enormous; in 1851–53 some 100 tons were used in New York Harbor alone to destroy Pot Rock, a large rock near the confluence of the East River and Harlem River. This last example deserves to be noted. High explosives are usually thought of as military weapons, but they also have immensely beneficial uses in mining, quarrying, and civil engineering. Surprisingly,

UNDERWATER EXPLOSIONS

Until the mid-nineteenth century, it was difficult for ships traveling the Atlantic Ocean to land at New York Harbor. To reach the city, they had to sail up Long Island Sound, passing through a narrow channel that was known as Hell Gate. This strait was near the point where the East River and the Harlem River met, and was characterized by strong currents. Several large underwater rocks in this area—known as Pot Rock, the Frying Pan, and Way's Reef—added to the danger. The currents and rocks of Hell Gate were notorious for causing ships to lose control and run aground or sink. By the 1850s, about 1,000 ships a year were damaged or sunk in Hell Gate.

The blasting of these rocks was one of the earliest examples within the U.S. Office of Coast Survey (now the National Oceanic and Atmospheric Administration, or NOAA) of a desire to modify the environment for human benefit. In 1848, Charles Henry Davis and David Dixon Porter suggested that Way's Reef, Pot Rock, and other rocks be removed from Hell Gate. Acting on this suggestion, a group of New York citizens hired a European engineer, Benjamin Maillefert, to blast rocks out of the channel. Between blasts, a Coast Survey hydrographic crew measured the changing depths and configuration of the rocks in the blasted areas. The nautical chart pictured here is the

gunpowder was still virtually the only explosive in use after 500 years. The only significant change had been in how the ingredients were mixed. From early in the fifteenth century, these were mixed wet instead of dry; apart from being safer, this "corned" powder was a more uniform and satisfactory material.

This, in brief, is the story of explosives up to the time of Alfred Nobel. In barely a quarter of a century, he was to transform an industry which had

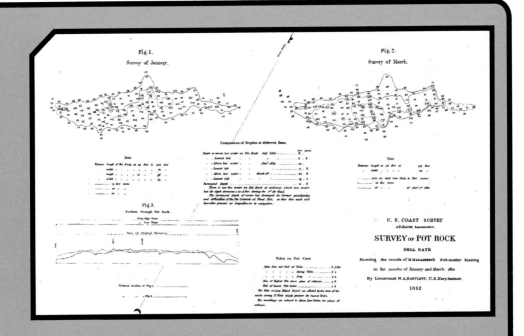

result of these surveying efforts between January and March 1852.

The work was not completed until after the end of the Civil War in 1865. Over 30,000 cubic feet of rock were removed at Pot Rock and its depth was increased from six feet to twenty feet. Other obstructions were removed during blasting, making Hell Gate safer for vessels traveling between the Hudson River and Long Island Sound.

hardly changed since medieval times. Meanwhile, however, the conditions for change were being established. In about 1845 Christian Friedrich Schönbein (1799–1868), professor of chemistry at the University of Basle, found that if cotton and other forms of nearly pure **cellulose** are treated with nitric acid, a highly explosive product called "guncotton" is formed. Its explosive power was so much greater than that of gunpowder that in 1846, Schönbein patented it in Britain, and manufacture was started in a gunpowder works at Faversham, Kent, England. Guncotton factories were also built in France and elsewhere in Europe. In the summer of 1847, there was a disastrous explosion at Faversham and twenty-one men were killed. No further attempt at producing guncotton was made in Britain at that time, and in Europe the dangerous work was continued only in Austria. Many years elapsed before Sir Frederick Abel (1827–1902) discovered how to make guncotton safe to handle.

At about the same time, another important discovery had been made in Italy. Ascanio Sobrero (1812–88), professor of chemistry at the University of Turin, had found in 1846 that a violently explosive oily liquid is produced by treating glycerine with nitric acid. However, this liquid explosive was too unreliable to use. It was Alfred Nobel who transformed a dangerous liquid chemical novelty into a safe and powerful explosive.

TEXT-DEPENDENT QUESTIONS

1. Why are Nobel Prizes awarded on December 10 each year?
2. The armies of what empire employed Greek Fire in warfare?
3. What was the first major European battle in which gunpowder was used?
4. What chemist developed guncotton in 1845?

RESEARCH PROJECT

Using your school library or the internet, do some research on the preparation of gunpowder prior to the nineteenth century. Write a two-page paper, describing where the materials needed were found, as well as the techniques that were used to prepare it. Share your findings with your class.

Traditional gothic buildings on Kornhamnstorg Square, near the harbor of Stockholm. Alfred Nobel was born in this Swedish city in 1833.

WORDS TO UNDERSTAND

nitrate—salt created by combining nitric acid with an inorganic base or an alcohol.

nitroglycerin ($C_2H_5(ONO_2)_3$)—an extremely explosive oily liquid produced by treating glycerine with nitric acid.

rector—a member of the clergy who has charge of a parish.

CHAPTER 2

Early Life

How much is a man's life determined by inherited qualities, and how much by environment and upbringing? These remain matters for heated argument. In Nobel's case both factors played a part. Although he came from quite humble parents, his great-great-great-grandfather was Olaf Rudbeck (1630–1702). Rudbeck was a gifted academic who became **rector** of Uppsala University; keenly interested in science and medicine, he is said to have discovered the lymphatic system. He also published a major archaeological work entitled *Atlantica*. His name is used for the genus of plants known as *Rudbeckia*.

Rudbeck's daughter Wendela married Petrus Oluffson, a law graduate of Uppsala University, who eventually became a judge. Their youngest son was Olaf Persson Nobelius (1706–60), a well-known painter of miniatures. Olaf's son, Alfred's grandfather, was Immanuel Nobelius (1757–1839). Immanuel was a doctor who changed his family name to Nobel during his military service. Clearly, there was no lack of talent among Alfred Nobel's forebears on his father's side.

Of his mother's family little is known, except that her name was Andriette Ahlsell and that she came from a south Swedish farming family. She was a devoted wife and mother, and Alfred was deeply attached to her.

Alfred's father was Immanuel Nobel (1801–72), a man who had certainly inherited his family's creative talents, but unfortunately had a notable lack of success in business. He was often away from home

Olaf Rudbeck, Alfred Nobel's illustrious fore-bear, who was rector of Uppsala University in the seventeenth century.

on speculative ventures. The family enjoyed an intellectually stimulating life, but their fortunes were erratic, and at times they suffered severe poverty. They were often on the move and none of the children had much formal education; Alfred had no more than a couple of years (1841–42) at school in Stockholm. Nevertheless, later he became an honorary graduate of Uppsala University, where his illustrious ancestor Rudbeck had been rector.

Immanuel Nobel's basic occupation is unknown. As a boy, he went to sea as a cabin boy, and on his return to Sweden began to study architecture. As a young man he seems to have survived mainly as a building contractor—with an unprofitable sideline as inventor. In 1833, one record describes him as an artist (though draftsman is probably more correct), and he was apparently bankrupt; the year before, the family home and all their possessions were destroyed by fire. Alfred was born in 1833, when his parents were in poor lodgings in Stockholm. He had two older brothers—Robert, born in 1829, and Ludwig, born in 1831—with whom, as we shall see, he was closely involved in various business enterprises. There were eight children, but only four survived to maturity. The youngest, Emil, died in tragic circumstances when he was only twenty-one.

In 1837, partly to escape his creditors and partly to seek his fortune elsewhere, Immanuel left his family in Stockholm and went to Finland as an architect and builder. No doubt he sent home what money he could, but for five years, the family's main support seems to have been a dairy and vegetable shop run by the mother. In about 1840 Immanuel went from Finland to St. Petersburg (now Leningrad) in Russia, and worked as an engineer. For a time he prospered and in 1842, when Alfred was a boy of nine, he was able to send for his family to join him in Russia. Not only could the creditors be paid in full, but there

Immanuel Nobel Jr, Alfred Nobel's father.

was even enough money to hire private tutors for the boys. One tutor was Nikolai Zinin (1811–80), a distinguished professor of chemistry.

Immanuel Nobel's Factory

The nature of Immanuel's work is important, for there is no doubt that it had a powerful effect on Alfred's career and on those of his brothers. While in Sweden, Immanuel's inventive genius had turned to making mines for military use on land and at sea, but the Swedish government showed little interest. In Russia things were different. Relations with the Western Powers were uneasy; Russia was looking to her armaments, and the Ministry of War invited Immanuel to demonstrate his mines on land and at sea and paid him a fee for his work. It appears to have been this fee that enabled him to establish his factory.

Immanuel Nobel's mines were used at sea during the Crimean War, which broke out in 1853, but it seems they served more as a deterrent than a destructive weapon. His artistic talent is shown in a beautifully illustrated manuscript that describes an elaborate system of maritime defense using mines. The war brought a flood of orders from the Russian government for guns, large marine steam engines, ships' propellers, and other heavy engineering products. To meet these pressing demands, Immanuel expanded his factory with borrowed money, relying on the promise of the government—which in 1853 had awarded him a gold medal for services to Russian industry—that he could depend on plenty of orders. But Emperor Nicholas I died during the war, and when peace was signed, the government abandoned Nobel and his factories and went back to placing most of its orders abroad.

Once again Immanuel was ruined, and he returned to Sweden. He had, however, an unsuspected asset in his three sons—Robert, Ludwig, and Alfred. The first two chose to remain in Russia, while Alfred gained valuable experience by traveling widely. The fourth son, Emil, who had been born in Russia, and was then only eighteen, returned with his parents to Stockholm.

As so often happens, the tide of fortune was turning just when things seemed at their worst. In St. Petersburg the two elder sons, Robert and Ludwig, applied themselves to salvaging what they could of the old business and embarking on new enterprises, including sawmills and a brickworks. In 1862 Robert, who had married a wealthy Finnish wife, left Russia to settle in Helsingfors. Shortly afterward, Ludwig embarked on an enterprise that was to be much more significant in the long run, the Aurora Lamp Oil Company. Initially, he was no more than a dealer but it gave him valuable experience of the petroleum industry, in which he and Alfred were later destined to play a very large role.

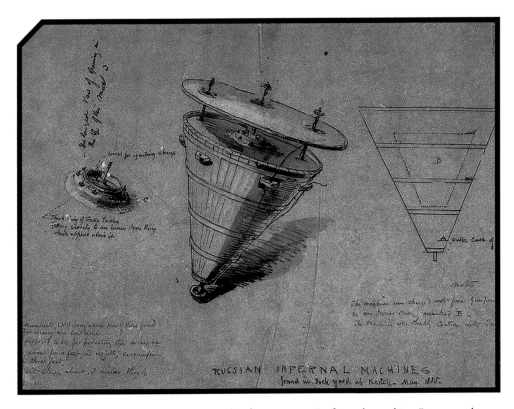

A British naval officer drew this sketch of a Russian "infernal machine"—or under-water mine—captured during a raid on the Russian port of Kertch. Immanuel Nobel manufactured similar devices for the Russians during the Crimean War.

We have little information about Alfred's life during these years. His education with his tutors in St. Petersburg probably ended about 1850, when he was seventeen years old. The family fortune was then sufficient to send him on extensive travels to complete his education as an engineer. Alfred visited the main cities of Europe, observing and studying. He seems to have spent some time working in Paris in the laboratory of the distinguished chemist T. J. Pelouze (1807–67). He also spent some time, perhaps two years (probably, 1850–52) in the United States. Here he met the brilliant Swedish engineer John Ericcson (1803–99), whose ironclad ship, the *Monitor*, played a decisive part in the Battle of Hampton Roads

T. J. PELOUZE

The French chemist Théophile-Jules Pelouze was the son of a respected French scientist. He was born in Valognes, a small town in Normandy. His talent helped him earn a position as chemistry professor at the École Polytechnique, one of the most prestigious research institutes in France. Pelouze held this position from 1831 until 1847. He also taught chemistry at Collège de France in Paris from 1831 to 1850.

The French chemist Théophile-Jules Pelouze.

In 1838, Pelouze discovered that paper or cardboard could be treated with nitric acid to create a lightweight, combustible explosive material. In 1846 he started an experimental laboratory and school, where he worked with explosive materials. Among his students were Ascanio Sobrero, who would discover nitroglycerin in 1847, and Alfred Nobel.

Pelouze did not only work with explosives. He did important research related to acids and fats that would be a major part of the modern science of organic chemistry. His importance as a scientist is indicated by the fact that, twenty years after Pelouze's death in 1867, the engineer Gustave Eiffel chose him as one of seventy-two French scientsts whose names are carved on the Eiffel Tower in Paris.

in 1862. It is doubtful, however, whether Alfred actually worked with Ericcson.

Surviving correspondence reminds us that he achieved so much in spite of lifelong ill-health. In the summer of 1854 he visited the health spa of Franzensbad to seek relief. He had to drive himself relentlessly, all the time.

Eventually he went back to St. Petersburg to join his brothers in the business there, and the experience gained through his travels made him a valuable asset. Not only had he had good training in engineering and chemistry, but he had studied foreign business

John Ericcson, the Swedish-American mechanical engineer, whose many achievements included the design of the Civil War warship Monitor.

methods. In addition he had a good command of German, English, French, and Russian.

Building a New Business

The story of Alfred's early life is very much the story of the Nobel family. When Immanuel Nobel returned to Stockholm after the collapse of his Russian business, he was sixty. He courageously set about building a new business and by 1863 was busy manufacturing a form of gunpowder that used sodium chlorate instead of the traditional **nitrate**. Optimistic as

Photograph of Alfred Nobel in the 1850s.

always, Immanuel visualized great sales for this product abroad, especially in Russia. He wrote to Alfred in St. Petersburg, urging him to return to Stockholm to help him.

This letter came at a good moment, for Alfred had himself developed a keen interest in explosives, trying to find a safe way of using Sobrero's **nitroglycerin**. He had learned something about this from his old tutor in St. Petersburg, Professor Zinin, and doubtless also from Pelouze in Paris. Also, much information about its manufacture and use had been published in the scientific journals, for all to read, by Sobrero, Pelouze, and others. When his father's letter arrived, Alfred had already prepared nitroglycerin and had successfully exploded small charges underwater. But his visit to Stockholm was a disappointment, for the new gunpowder failed to live up to its promise.

It turned out that Immanuel, too, had been experimenting with nitroglycerin and had tried to make it safer and more manageable by mixing it with gunpowder to produce a sort of dough. Although the mixture was more powerful than gunpowder, it fell far short of the explosive potential of the nitroglycerin contained in it.

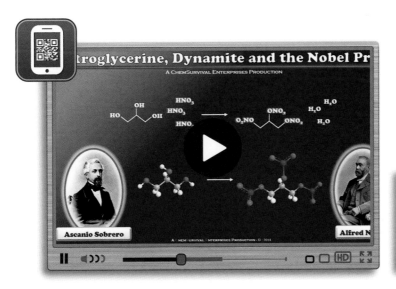

Scan here to learn more about nitroglycerin:

Alfred had also been looking at the possibility of combining gunpowder and nitroglycerin, but in a quite different way. Nitroglycerin is a treacherous substance. Although very inflammable, its burning does not always lead to an explosion; it may just burn away with a bright flame, like alcohol. It is only when the combustion gets out of hand, as it were, that the dramatically explosive properties reveal themselves. For practical use, this variability is a grave disadvantage. Apart from wanting an explosion of predictable force every time, the civil or military engineer never wants to have a quantity of unexploded material left on his hands that is unsafe to handle. Alfred realized that while sudden heat might detonate nitroglycerin, this could be done more reliably by a sharp shock whose waves would permeate the whole of the material. To obtain this shock, he used gunpowder, itself exploded by a detonator. Although apparently simple, this was a decisive invention and it paved the way to the successful exploitation of nitroglycerin, which Nobel regarded as his greatest achievement.

This success was not immediate, however. At first, the new discovery started a quarrel between father and son. Immanuel, not realizing that this use of gunpowder was in principle quite different from his own, accused his son of claiming the discovery as his own. In a polite, but very sharp, letter, Alfred defended his position and his father recognized that the credit for the discovery, and the valuable patent relating to it, was Alfred's alone.

Sometime in the latter part of 1863, father and son set up a small works at Heleneborg, near their home in Stockholm, for making nitroglycerin. Alfred's youngest brother, Emil—still only twenty years old—was also employed in the works. For a year all went well and small quantities of nitroglycerin were sold for quarrying, mining, and railway construction. Then, on September 3, 1864, there was a violent explosion. Emil and four workmen were killed. The precise cause was never known, but it is possible that Emil, with the best of motives, had departed from the prescribed process of manufacture.

The disaster was, of course, a grievous loss to the Nobel family, and soon afterward, Immanuel suffered a severe stroke. He lived until 1872, and

A stage in the manufacture of nitroglycerin by the early batch method. The workman sits on a one-legged stool—a device to ensure that he would be wakened should he nod off as he watched the thermometer during a critical stage of the process.

recovered his mental faculties, but his remaining years were those of an invalid.

In these tragic circumstances, the whole burden of the burgeoning Swedish nitroglycerin industry fell on Alfred. The problems before him were considerable. The Heleneborg disaster aroused great public indignation and he had a hard time justifying carrying out such a dangerous procedure in a populous area. For a long time he could find no other site within the city area, even though there was still a pressing demand for the product, especially to complete the last stage of the state railway into Stockholm. Eventually an acceptable solution was found by manufacturing on a barge anchored on Malar Lake, near Stockholm.

Production was still on a small scale for local use, and was in the hands of the Nitro-Glycerine Company founded by Alfred and Immanuel Nobel, in collaboration with others. Not until March 1865 was the world's first real high explosives factory established at Winterwick, near Stockholm. The manufacturing process was very simple. It really amounted to no more than a scaled-up version of Sobrero's laboratory process. The use of pumps and other machinery was deliberately avoided, to eliminate the possibility of excessive local heating through friction or other causes and the accumulation of pockets of dangerous material. The plant was arranged so that the liquid reagents and products flowed by gravity.

At this time, more than a century ago, many people had little understanding of the nature of nitroglycerin. Often it was treated in an appallingly casual way. It was generally transported to the point where it was used in small cans or bottles packed in wooden crates. If some were broken or spilled on the way, no one worried. On one occasion, oil that had leaked was used to lubricate a cart, and on another, to rehydrate the leather of a harness. However, luck did not always favor the ignorant or foolhardy. The early manufacture and use of the explosive caused so many fatal accidents that the very existence of the new industry was threatened.

TEXT-DEPENDENT QUESTIONS

1. Why did Immanuel Nobel leave his family in Stockholm in 1837?

2. When did Alfred Nobel's education with tutors in St. Petersburg end?

3. What chemist developed nitroglycerin?

 RESEARCH PROJECT

Using your school library or the internet, find out more about the Swedish-American inventor John Ericsson. Write a two-page paper about his life and accomplishments, and share it with your class.

The Nobel factory at Ardeer, Scotland, in 1897. Before entering the danger zone, workers were searched to make sure that they were not carrying metallic objects, which might give rise to sparks and cause a massive explosion.

 WORDS TO UNDERSTAND

ballistite—a mixture of nitrocotton and nitroglycerin that burns well and is a good propellant.

blasting gelatin—a mixture basically of nitroglycerin and nitrocellulose perfected by Nobel in 1875; relatively stable, its explosiveness can be varied by altering the proportions of the two ingredients.

cordite—a smokeless explosive similar to ballistite, but with the addition of some acetone and petroleum jelly to make it more stable. It can be extruded in the form of cords and, if desired, chopped into pellets.

dynamite—a highly explosive but relatively safe mixture of nitroglycerin and kieselguhr patented by Nobel in 1867.

kieselguhr—a very porous form of clay which, when mixed with nitroglycerin, produces dynamite.

methyl alcohol (CH_3OH)—a simple form of alcohol distilled from wood. It can be used to produce a chemical reaction.

CHAPTER 3

An International Business

Up to the founding of the Winterwick factory in 1865, Alfred Nobel's nitroglycerin operations had been entirely Swedish. He soon decided that the business must be developed internationally, and during the next decade, factories were established throughout Europe and in North America. Production near the site where it would be used had obvious economic advantages, particularly with a material needing such careful handling. Nevertheless, from the early days quite a big export business was built up by many of the factories.

Nobel's first factory outside Sweden was built at Krümmel, on the River Elbe near Hamburg, in 1865. By 1873 he had also opened works in Norway, Finland, Bohemia, Scotland, France, Spain, Switzerland, Italy, Portugal and Hungary. In 1868 came the first big American venture: the Giant Powder Company in San Francisco. However, these ventures were fraught with danger and the advice of Alfred Nobel, as the expert on nitroglycerin, was sought all the time.

A series of accidents troubled the whole industry. The worst occurred in 1866, when the steamship *European* blew up with the loss of seventy-four lives. Almost simultaneously, fourteen lives were lost in an explosion in a warehouse in San Francisco. In the same year, the Krümmel factory was destroyed and there was a big explosion in Sydney, Australia. Public feeling ran high and many countries either banned the manufacture of nitroglycerin altogether or restricted its transport and use so severely as to have virtually the same effect.

Safety Improvements

Despite all his business cares, and almost constant travel, Alfred Nobel gave much attention to making nitroglycerin safe to use without weakening its explosive force. At first, he pinned his hopes to the process of adding **methyl alcohol** to the manufactured product; this much reduced its readiness to explode and could easily be washed out with water immediately before use. It was, however, a troublesome arrangement and he experimented with mixing nitroglycerin with some inert material that would produce a solid product.

He may well have been influenced by his father's early experiments in mixing nitroglycerin with gunpowder, and by knowing that nitroglycerin

Dynamite would become Alfred Nobel's most famous invention.

leaking from containers sometimes formed a paste with the powder in which they were packed. But there is no doubt that Nobel's new invention arose, not from chance, but from thinking about the basic principles involved. After trying all kinds of absorbents—including charcoal, cement, and brick-dust—he finally found the ideal in a common form of clay known as **kieselguhr**, which is particularly porous. He patented the use of this in 1867 and from then on began to manufacture **dynamite**, as the mixture of kieselguhr and nitroglycerin was called. Despite the clear advantages of the new product, it was some thirty years before the more conservative mining companies, especially in Sweden, finally stopped asking for liquid nitroglycerin.

The new dynamite profoundly changed the fortunes of the troubled nitroglycerin industry. Production rose rapidly and within five years multiplied several hundred times. When Nobel addressed the Society of Arts in London in 1875, he told his audience that the sale of dynamite in the previous year had exceeded 3,000 tons. This compared with 424 tons in 1870 and only 11 tons in 1867. These figures, which appeared very impressive then, are of course far lower than today's sales.

Dynamite was a great improvement, but it still was not quite satisfactory. The dilution with inert kieselguhr diminished the explosive force of the nitroglycerin. Also, the product was liable to "sweat" and exude dangerous drops of liquid nitroglycerin. In the end, Nobel found a way of mixing nitroglycerin with guncotton or nitrocellulose. The secret of his success lay in using cotton (or some other form of cellulose) that was less highly nitrated than usual. His product—**blasting gelatin**—was perfected in 1875. Its explosive properties and consistency could be adjusted by varying the proportions of the two ingredients; generally the nitrocellulose content lay between 2.5 and 7 percent.

All these types of explosives were primarily suited for general rock blasting, and in this field, the supremacy of gunpowder was quickly destroyed. Dynamite, for example, is about five times more powerful than gunpowder. For other purposes, especially for the military, gunpowder was much less

Blasting with dynamite or other high explosives is still used in both open pit and underground mining operations.

easily replaced. Alfred Nobel explained why in his lecture to the Society of Arts in 1875:

> It is difficult, even with more powerful explosives at command, to supersede gunpowder. That old mixture possesses a truly admirable elasticity which permits its adaptation to purposes of the most varied nature. Thus, in a mine, it is wanted to blast without propelling; in a gun to propel without blasting; in a shell it serves both purposes combined; in a fuse, as in fireworks, it burns quite slowly without exploding. Its pressure, exercised in these numerous operations, varies between one ounce (more or less) to the square inch, in a fuse and 85,000 lbs to the square inch in a shell.

Improving Gunpowder

For military purposes a smokeless explosive was wanted. It would not give away the position of artillery in action, and would cause less fouling of the gun barrel. Several inventors applied themselves to this. The first to achieve success was Major J. F. E. Schultze (1825–74) of the Prussian Artillery, who in about 1865 introduced a powder based on nitrated wood mixed with saltpeter. This was suitable for artillery and shotguns, but too violent for rifles. Schultze powder was manufactured in England from 1868.

Another kind of smokeless powder was invented in 1882 by W. F. Reid and D. Johnson, at the Explosives Company at Stowmarket, England. In granular form, it was based on nitrocotton mixed with saltpeter and partially gelatinized with a mixture of alcohol and ether. Again, it was too powerful for rifles. In France, P. M. E. Vieille (1854–1934) developed an explosive based on fully gelatinized nitrocotton. The dough-like material was rolled into thin sheets, diced, and dried. It was known as Poudre B (a tribute to General E. J. M. Boulanger (1837–91), at that time in command of the army of occupation in Tunis).

Scan here for a short video on the origins of gun-powder:

Case for a rocket powered by ballistite, designed by Alfred Nobel and W. T. Unge, 1896.

Alfred Nobel now made his contribution, with the introduction of **ballistite** in 1888. The development was both new and surprising. Nobel had found that if nitrocotton and nitroglycerin are mixed, each violent partner seems to tame the other. The mixture does not explode so much as burn ferociously, but with great regularity. It therefore makes a good propellant. Experience showed that some other ingredients, such as camphor, improved the explosive characteristics.

Yet ballistite was to cause Nobel much disappointment. In 1869, the British government had passed an Act of Parliament virtually banning the use of nitroglycerin, or preparations containing it, such as dynamite. Nobel regarded this as discrimination and largely put it down to prejudice on the part of Sir Frederick Abel (1827–1902), the British government's chief adviser on explosives, in favor of guncotton. Abel had made the major discovery that guncotton could be stabilized by extremely thorough washing to remove every trace of acid. Eventually the quarrel was made up and

Nobel and Abel became good friends. Unfortunately, the discovery of ballistite was to revive the quarrel.

In 1888, the British government set up an Explosives Commission to advise it on the best use of the new discoveries in this field, especially in the military context. Abel was a member of this Commission, and in close touch with Nobel, who was very frank with him. The Commission expressed doubts about ballistite, mainly because the camphor in it was volatile and so would gradually disappear. Nobel suggested various ways of eliminating this defect.

The Cordite Affair

Meanwhile, however, Abel, together with another distinguished chemist Sir James Dewar (1842–1923), had developed and patented a modification containing a little acetone and petroleum jelly. This was named **cordite**: it was plastic enough to be extruded through a die in the form of cord, which could then be chopped into pellets. Abel and Dewar transferred their English patent rights to the British government, but retained—and exercised—the rights of exploitation abroad. Understandably Nobel regarded this as an infringement of his own patent and protested strongly. Since he received no satisfaction, it was agreed to institute "friendly" proceedings so that the case could be argued formally in the British courts. The case lasted two years (1893–95), going to the Court of Appeal and then to the House of Lords. The verdict finally went against Nobel, mainly because of an alleged looseness of expression in the drafting of his own patent. The suit cost Nobel £28,000 and left him very embittered.

Elsewhere, too, ballistite landed Nobel in serious trouble. The first government to take it up was the Italian, who in 1889 placed an initial contract for some 300 tons with its Avigliana factory; Nobel was to receive a royalty. Soon afterward, the Italian government concluded an exclusive royalty agreement with Nobel. This caused a strong reaction in France, where Nobel was then living, because the French government was strongly backing Vieille's smokeless powder, to which Nobel's product was a serious

Sir Frederick Abel (left) and Sir James Dewar modified Nobel's formula for ballistite, creating a smokeless propellant that they called cordite. Nobel sued for patent infringement, but the British courts ultimately ruled in favor of the English scientists.

rival. As a result of this, Nobel's laboratory in Paris was shut down, his factory at Honfleur had to suspend its operations, and he was denied vital testing facilities. In 1891 Nobel, disillusioned, left France and went to live, for the five remaining years of his life, in Italy, mainly in San Remo.

In one way or another, these were all years of prodigious activity. Apart from spending much time in the laboratory making and developing his inventions, Nobel had quickly built up a complex international manufacturing and marketing organization. He had his own factories in the major countries of the world, he made reciprocal manufacturing arrangements with other companies, and appointed agents in other countries. Although part of one industrial empire, each company had a life and loyalty of its own and clashes of interest were by no means uncommon. Another cause of trouble was that involvement in politics was unavoidable because of the nature of the business. As the man with his finger on the pulse of the whole concern, as well as being the technical expert, Nobel was constantly in demand to resolve problems. This intervention was inescapable, but against his better judgment. In a letter to his brother Robert in 1883 he wrote: "We must confine ourselves to the work of thinking, and leave all the mechanics to others."

Eventually most of the business was arranged in two large trust companies. One, the Nobel Dynamite Trust Company, in London, concerned itself mainly with the British and German interests. The other, the Société Centrale de Dynamite, in Paris, looked after the French, Swiss, Italian, South American, and certain other interests. As the enterprise grew, so did the number of associates on whom Nobel was dependent, and he was not always fortunate in his choice. Indeed, one of them, Paul Barbe, seemed at one time to have ruined him utterly. Paul Barbe and his father were ironfounders near Nancy and in 1868, Nobel signed an agreement with them to market his explosive products in France. Barbe was exceptionally gifted and industrious, and for many years the partnership worked well. Unfortunately, Barbe was also unscrupulous and politically very ambitious. Nobel knew this, but believed that the weakness could be contained and was far outweighed by Barbe's exceptional abilities.

In 1883, he wrote to his brother Robert about Barbe, saying: "He has a marvellous scientific imagination, is an exceptionally good salesman, a far-seeing business man, and knows how to make the best of people and to get out of each man the individual work of which he is capable. His own achievements are as incredible as his power to work; but he is unreliable unless his personal interest is involved. This is a hateful defect. . ." Barbe realized his political ambition—which was, of course, very helpful to Nobel in his dealings with the French government—and at the time of his death in 1890, had for some years been Minister of Agriculture. After his death, however, it was found that Barbe had been implicated in the notorious

San Remo, Italy, where Nobel spent the last five years of his life.

Panama Scandal and some of his associates in the Société Centrale de Dynamite had speculated unsuccessfully in glycerin using the company's money. For a time, Nobel contemplated the necessity of becoming an employee in his own business in Germany, because of these financial difficulties, but in the end his resources, and resourcefulness, were enough to save the situation.

In the United States, too, his experience was not happy. There one of his associates, T. P. Shaffner, proved treacherous and tried to rob Nobel of his patent rights in the use of nitroglycerin. Long and costly litigation was needed to restore the situation. Booming development in America greatly increased the demand for explosives, but there was strong opposition from established gunpowder manufacturers, especially the powerful firm of Du Pont de Nemours at Wilmington. Generally speaking the business was more troublesome than profitable, and Nobel withdrew from his American interests altogether in 1885.

For a man in robust health, the constant travel, meetings, and anxieties connected with the rapid establishment of a large worldwide enterprise would have been exhausting enough. That a man whose health had been frail from childhood should have done so much is remarkable. Yet more remarkable is the fact that, in addition, he not only managed some very large enterprises of a quite different kind, but was also an active worker in the cause of international peace. These other facets of the character of this exceptional man we must now consider.

TEXT-DEPENDENT QUESTIONS

1. Where was Alfred Nobel's first explosives factory outside of Sweden built?
2. What did Nobel blend with nitroglycerin to create dynamite?
3. What smokeless gunpowder did Nobel introduce in 1888?
4. What British chemists developed cordite, which Nobel considered an infringement on his patent?

RESEARCH PROJECT

Many people use the terms "TNT" and "dynamite" interchangeably, but is there a difference between these two high explosives? Using your school library or the internet, find out more about trinitrotoluene (TNT, or the chemical compound $C_6H_2(NO_2)_3CH_3$). Write a short paper comparing the two types of explosives. What are some important differences? Which is more powerful? Share your findings with your class.

During the late nineteenth century, the Nobel family helped to develop the international oil industry. Here, black oil gushes high above the earth after an early strike in an underdeveloped oil field.

WORDS TO UNDERSTAND

electrochemical works—a factory where batteries are produced.

pipeline—a long pipe used for conveying oil or gas over long distances.

profit-sharing scheme—a plan in which the people who work for a company receive a direct share of the profits.

CHAPTER 4

Nobel and the Petroleum Industry

Alfred's older brother Ludwig stayed behind in St. Petersburg after their father went back to Stockholm. Ludwig applied himself to making a living as an engineer. At first he worked for the creditors as a salaried employee of the old family business, responsible for winding it up. Before long, however, he was back in business on his own account as a manufacturing engineer. Ludwig began to make artillery and other firearms, and converted muzzle-loading muskets into breech-loaders. In this business he was rejoined by his brother Robert in 1870. Later, in 1878, he worked on a major contract to provide 450,000 rifles for the Russian government. Surprisingly, it was this work that led the brothers into the oil business.

Traditionally, good rifle butts are made of walnut, and Robert went to the Caucasus to see whether he could buy the wood there. Some wood was obtained, though not enough. But on this trip Robert saw for himself how petroleum was being extracted and processed at Baku on the Caspian Sea. Though still very primitive, the petroleum industry was an old one, and had been described by Marco Polo, who visited Baku in 1272. Russia had acquired the oil-producing regions from Persia in 1806.

When he got back to St. Petersburg, Robert persuaded Ludwig to help him set up a Caspian oil business. The enterprise was a great success. Despite the rough terrain, their lack of knowledge of the business, and the hostility of other operators, the business grew with remarkable speed. The brothers

For a short history of the oil industry in the Caspian Sea region, scan here:

A Nobel Brothers office and horse-drawn tanker carriage near Baku, circa 1885. At one point the Nobel Brothers' company in the Russian Empire, Branobel, produced 50 percent of the world's oil.

introduced all kinds of new techniques: oil **pipelines**, tanker ships for conveying the oil by sea or river, rail tank-cars to transport it by land. More remarkable, for the times, was their attitude toward their workers. Near their works they built a "garden city," with houses for the workers set in the parkland with a range of libraries, billiard halls, and other public buildings for recreation, and schools for the children. Recognizing that the success of any business depends on the loyalty and enthusiasm of its workers, the brothers started a workers' **profit-sharing scheme**, almost unheard of in those days. To encourage thrift, a savings bank was established.

Ludwig Nobel (1831–88) is credited with creating the oil industry in Russia. He was the first president of Branobel.

Yet there were great difficulties, especially in raising the necessary funds. It was in this connection that Alfred once again became closely involved with his two elder brothers. As early as 1875, Ludwig had written to Alfred hoping to persuade him to visit Baku, but for a long time Alfred preferred to watch the development of the business from a distance. In 1877 the two brothers met in Paris, and in the following year agreed to form the Nobel Brothers' Naphtha Company; the articles of association were formally approved by the Emperor of Russia in the following year.

An oilfield complex, probably with worker housing, near Branobel wells at the Balakhani field in the Russian Empire (modern-day Azerbaijan) during the 1890s.

At first, Alfred's holding was a modest 10 percent, but this increased over the years as the company raised new capital to finance its phenomenally rapid expansion. In 1883 he became a director for a short time, mainly to curb what he regarded as over-spending. By 1898 the company had grown so fast that it had a fleet of no less than fifty-three tankers, capable of carrying 80,000 tons of oil. The tankers had been built in Sweden and brought through an elaborate system of inland waterways from the Baltic Sea to the Caspian Sea; the largest had to be built in two parts in order to negotiate the locks. Vast storage tanks had to be built, partly because of the seasonal nature of the business. At that time, before the advent of the gas-powered automobile, the main usage was as lamp oil, and naturally the demand for this was greatest during the dark winter months. On the technical side Ludwig showed the same flair and compulsive urge to work as Alfred did on the financial side.

Although explosives and petroleum were Alfred Nobel's main industrial interests, his restless mind turned itself in many other directions and in the course of his lifetime he filed more than 350 patents. These ranged over such diverse fields as artificial fibers, synthetic rubber, paints based on nitrocellulose, sound reproduction, and artificial gems. Late in life, in 1895, he founded

Robert Nobel (1829–96) was the oldest of the Nobel brothers, and the first to become involved in the oil industry in Baku.

an **electrochemical works** in Sweden with engineer Rudolf Lilljeqvist, who was to be one of the executors of his will. Nobel had interests in the manufacture of bicycles, boilers, and turbines. At one time he became interested in blood transfusion. He even helped to finance S. A. Andrée's ill-fated attempt to reach the North Pole in a balloon in 1897. He clearly foresaw, however, that the future of aviation lay not in balloons but in mechanically propelled aircraft: "We must not think of solving this problem by means of balloons…. We have to have floating rafts driven forward at great speed."

In 1894, in spite of increasingly frequent heart attacks, Nobel set off on yet another journey. He first visited London, where an appeal to the House of Lords was being prepared in the cordite case, and then went on to Sweden. His objective was to establish a works in Sweden suitable for the manufacture of modern armaments, and in pursuit of this he visited the Bofors-Gullsprång Company, owners of a steelworks at Bofors, in which he had a majority shareholding. Bofors suited his needs very well, and it was here that many of the speculative experiments mentioned above were carried out. Close by, at Björkborn, he bought a fine country house as a residence in the summer months, wintering in San Remo in Italy. The remote location suited him in many ways: it was away from the turmoil of Paris, where he had been so harassed, and from the irritation of San Remo, where his neighbors had objected to his noisy ballistic experiments. It also gave him a footing in his native country once again, to which in his later years his sympathies were increasingly turning after long years of travel and self-imposed exile. He once called himself the richest vagabond in Europe.

The first oil tanker, Zoroaster, was constructed in Sweden for Branobel Oil and launched in 1878.

TEXT-DEPENDENT QUESTIONS

1. In what region did Robert and Ludwig Nobel establish an oil business?
2. How many patents did Alfred Nobel hold in his lifetime?
3. In what Swedish village did Nobel spend his summers?

RESEARCH PROJECT

Using your school library or the internet, find out more about the development of the petroleum industry in the nineteenth century. Where was oil discovered, and what was it used for? How were new inventions and innovations developed to take advantage of this resource? Write a two-page report and share it with your class.

Alfred Nobel in his home at San Remo, Italy.

WORDS TO UNDERSTAND

intrigue—the secret planning of something that is illegal or detrimental to others.

ostentatious—characterized by vulgar or pretentious display.

self-deprecation—the act of belittling, undervaluing, or disparaging oneself, or being excessively modest.

CHAPTER 5

Nobel the Man

What was Alfred Nobel like as a person? This is already implied in the things he did; thus we are already acquainted with a man with a powerful and wide-ranging intellect, a flair for finance, a huge capacity for work, determination in the face of difficulties, and a strong sense of family unity. Much more than this can, however, be inferred from other evidence, for we know something of Nobel's estimation of himself, and others have left recorded views of him. Neither type of evidence, of course, is to be too heavily relied upon, for there is always the danger of self-deception or prejudice. Yet he was such a mass of contradictions that no simple interpretation of his personality is convincing.

One thread that certainly runs through Nobel's life is that of loneliness, and this explains many of the things he did. His loneliness was not that of the recluse, for he was always in contact with a large number of people. Rather was it the loneliness that comes from the inability to form close human relationships, and a reluctance to delegate. He had a wide circle of acquaintances but few friends. He once referred to "chance acquaintances, with whom one can, of course, spend a few pleasant hours, but from whom one later parts with as much regret as from an old worn-out coat."

Although by no means indifferent to women, he never married. In 1887 he wrote, "For the past nine days I have been ill and have had to stay indoors with no other company than a paid valet. . . . When at the age of fifty-four one is left so alone in the world, and a paid servant is the only person who has so far showed one the most kindness, then come heavy thoughts,

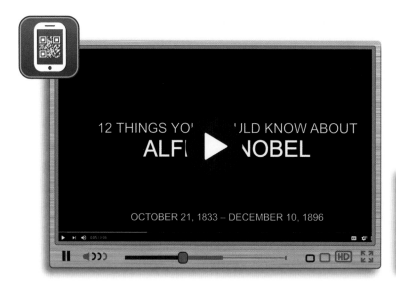

12 THINGS YO'_____'JLD KNOW ABOUT
ALF[▶ NOBEL

OCTOBER 21, 1833 – DECEMBER 10, 1896

Scan here to learn some facts about Alfred Nobel:

heavier than most people can imagine." He lived alone, and he died alone.

Possibly one cause of his loneliness was his chronic ill health, which even in childhood cut him off from many everyday activities. From about 1889, his heart trouble became serious. It probably made him even more self-sufficient. He also had the Swedish tendency to melancholy. Certainly he was given at times to self-pity. Thus in a letter to his sister-in-law, he contrasts her happy family life with his own loneliness: "I, drifting about with no compass or helm like a useless wreck battered by fate, without bright memories from the past, without the false but beautiful light of illusion for the future. . . ."

An Aloof Life

A detached look at Nobel's life does not really engender much sympathy for this sort of pleading, for so far as it was true, it was of his own making. Although he was meticulous in his family relationships, remembering anniversaries by writing and gifts, even this seems—except in the case of his mother, to whom he was devoted—to have been somewhat impersonal.

When Alfred Nobel acquired Bofors-Gullspång in 1894, the Björkborn Manor was part of the purchase. Alfred chose to live here during his visits to Sweden in the summer months, and conducted experiments at the nearby armaments factory between 1894 and 1896.

When he was aroused, his temper could be fierce but it quickly subsided. His wealth permitted him to live where and as he pleased. His home, wherever it might be, was well appointed and well served. He never smoked or drank, but his guests were always well looked after in these respects. In his dress he was not **ostentatious** but always neat and appropriate.

Although a celebrity in his own time, Nobel was invariably modest and given to **self-deprecation**; his instinct was always to remain in the

Nobel drew much inspiration from the Romantic-era poet Percy Bysshe Shelley (1792–1822).

background. He hated purely social gatherings and so far as he could, without giving offense, declined all public honors. Sarcastically, he once said that he owed his Swedish Order of the North Star to his cook, who had once pleased an influential stomach. He never sat for his portrait. Once, when he was asked for a picture to appear in some anniversary publication of one of his works, he refused unless every single workman was asked to do the same, saying, "Then I will send a reproduction of my pig's-bristle bachelor snout, not before."

He had to keep in touch with political events, because he constantly had to engage in negotiations with strong political overtones, but he never hid his contempt for politics as such. He regarded them as mainly a platform for **intrigue** and self-advancement. Perhaps this modesty was to some extent deliberately assumed, but of its practical consequences there is no doubt. With Swedish realism, Nobel knew the importance of social life, even though it gave him little personal pleasure. He once wrote, "He who withdraws himself from all cultured society, and neglects to keep alive the interchange of ideas with thoughtful persons, finally loses the capacity to do so."

Nobel the Writer

We have seen that ordinary relaxation found little place in Alfred Nobel's life. He had no interest in music, but he did find solace in literature, both as a reader and, more particularly, as a writer. In his reading, he preferred idealistic and imaginative writers to those who were descriptive. He had, of course, to do a tremendous amount of writing in his business, but apart from this, he had to his credit a number of purely literary compositions that are not without merit. The earliest, a poem in English of 425 lines, is of interest for the biographical information it provides on his early years, and the light it throws on his attitude to life. Considering that he was only eighteen when he wrote it, and his native language was Swedish, it is a very remarkable achievement.

"This breathing clay, what business has it here?
Some petty wants to chain us to the earth.
Some lofty thoughts to lift us to the spheres
And cheat us with that semblance of a soul,
To dream of immortality ..."

This command of poetic English is in striking contrast with his poor showing with Swedish prose. An unfinished novel, titled *Brothers and Sisters*, which Nobel probably wrote when he was about thirty, is almost totally lacking in merit. Certainly he was most successful with poetry, and perhaps this reflects the inventive genius of his mind, which was the basis of his success in business. It would seem that he often turned to writing as some sort of solace during a period of ill health or business anxiety. Thus the outcome of the great cordite case in England inspired a bitingly sarcastic comedy, called *The Patent Bacillus*, which he never completed.

In his poetry Nobel was much influenced by Percy Bysshe Shelley, and at the end of his life he set himself to write in Swedish a tragedy in four acts entitled *Nemesis*. Its theme, like Shelley's *The Cenci* (1819), is the life of the depraved fifteenth-century Roman nobleman, Francesco Cenci, who treated his four sons with abominable cruelty and debauched his daughter Beatrice. In Nobel's version the incestuous relationship with Beatrice is eliminated by making it appear that Cenci was not her father. The play was on the point of publication at the time of Nobel's death, and was suppressed by his family on the grounds that it would do him no credit. By the standards of the late nineteenth century, it would have been regarded as outspoken and Nobel himself was worried about the attitude of the Swedish censor. Today, however, it would be regarded as quite harmless. It seems, from the three copies that survived, that publication would certainly have done him no harm.

Alfred Nobel was not a man of deep religious conviction, but he certainly subscribed to basic Christian principles. A Lutheran by upbringing, he actively supported the Swedish Church in Paris while he lived there. To its pastor, Nathan Soderblom—later Archbishop of Sweden—he once wrote, "The difference in our religious views is perhaps formal rather than real, for we both agree that we should do to our neighbor what we want him to do to us." Characteristically, he could not refrain from going on to make a dig at himself: "Admittedly I go a step further, for I have a loathing for myself which I by no means have for my neighbor."

Inevitably, he was the recipient of a large number of begging letters, many from women. He once said that these averaged more than 100 a week, with demands totaling tens of thousands of dollars. Most deservedly received a blunt reply, but there were many who had cause to remember his generosity, which was always unobtrusively expressed.

Nobel the Peacemaker

In his later years, Nobel took an active part in the cause of world peace through his encouragement of various peace movements. But he had been interested in this cause for a long time. To some extent, no doubt, this was stimulated by his long-standing admiration for Shelley, who had strong pacifist views. To some, Nobel's championship of peace is a sign of hypocrisy—a symptom of an uneasy conscience in a man who had made

Bertha von Suttner (1843–1914), Nobel's secretary for a short period in 1876, later became well known as an ardent advocate for world peace.

such terrible weapons of destruction. Plausibly, and more charitably, it may be seen as another aspect of his difficulty over personal relationships; while individual men (and women) were a problem to him, he could be enthusiastic about mankind as a whole and about peace as an abstract idea.

Nobel was in touch with many of the pacifist leaders of his time, and much has been made of his relationship with Bertha von Suttner, an Austrian writer and worker for peace who had briefly worked as his secretary. He had no patience with impractical ideals. "What we need," he wrote in

PEACE CONFERENCES

Between 1803 and 1815, European countries were involved in a series of devastating conflicts known as the Napoleonic Wars. The Congress of Vienna, a peace conference that ended the wars, redrew the borders of Europe and attempted to end future conflicts by creating a balance of power through a system of international law. Some people came to believe that, through negotiation, future wars could be avoided altogether. In Europe and the United States, pacifists formed societies dedicated to ending war, such as the London Peace Society, formed in 1816, and the American Peace Society formed in 1815 in New York.

In order to promote the peace movement, and to create a platform from which it could develop an international program, the peace societies started to organize meetings of like-minded pacifists from all over the world, called "peace congresses." The first Peace Congress was held in London in 1843. Others were held in Brussels, Paris, Frankfurt, and other major European cities between 1848 and 1853. They attracted intellectuals, businessmen, lawyers, clergymen, and politicians.

1891, "is not money but a programme." His own plan was essentially one of political agreement between the great powers. All would unite against one that broke the peace. By such a means a prolonged period of peace might be assured and then, and only then, a progressive disarmament plan might be politically feasible. Meanwhile, armaments might serve better to preserve peace than "resolutions, banquets, and long speeches." Prophetically, he looked forward to "the day when two army corps will be able to destroy each other in one second [and] all civilized nations will recoil from war in horror and disband their armies." With atomic weapons,

However, the peace congresses failed to end wars. In October 1853, the Crimean War began; involving the Russian Empire, France, Britain, and the Ottoman Empire, more than 785,000 died before the war ended in 1856. The American Civil War (1861–65) presented a dilemna for pacifists: those who saw slavery as a greater evil than war supported the Union military effort, while others protested against violence in all circumstances.

In 1889, a French politician named Frédéric Passy founded the Inter-Parliamentary Union, an organization dedicated to peace. That year the Inter-Parliamentary Union held the first major international Peace Congress since 1853, in Paris. It was the first in a series of Universal Peace Congresses. Subsequent Universal Peace Congresses were held in London (1890), Rome (1891), Bern (1892), Chicago (1893), Antwerp (1894), and Budapest (1896). After this, congresses continued to be held regularly until 1913. The First World War, which began in 1914, put such meetings on hold until 1921. Peace congresses were thereafter held in most years from 1921 until the outbreak of the Second World War in 1939.

this fearful threat has become reality; how far such weapons of mass destruction have contributed to the avoidance of another world war can only be a matter of opinion.

The Peace Congress at Bern, Switzerland, in 1892 seems to have been something of a turning point in Nobel's ideas. Although he attended only briefly, it was long enough for him to form an decisive opinion. "I was astonished no less by the rapidly increasing number of able and serious members than by the ridiculous efforts made by gasbags, which must spoil the best cause," he wrote. "To demand disarmament or unconditional arbitration is, in the present State of mind of the persons in power, to incur the responsibility of putting forward ridiculous proposals which cannot be of the slightest use to anyone."

As his own contribution, he determined in 1893 to leave part of his fortune to a prize periodically awarded "to the man or woman who had done most to advance the idea of general peace in Europe." We shall see later how he carried out this intention.

Nobel and Women

No account of Nobel's life would be complete without some mention of the part women played in it. Here, he had none of the success that marked his business ventures, or the story of his life might have been very different. Apart from his mother, for whom he had a deep and lasting affection until her death in 1889, only seven years before his own, there were three women who were important in his life. The first we cannot identify, but she is explicitly mentioned in the biographical poem from which we have already quoted. As this was probably written about 1851, it is likely that it was a girl he met as a young student in Paris. Tragically, she died as their love blossomed:

"This might have ended in the usual manner
And brought the joys and griefs of wedded life;
But 'twas not so ordained; another bridegroom
Had stronger claims—she's wedded to her grave."

The central square in Baden bei Wien at evening. While visiting this small spa-town near Vienna in 1876, Nobel met Sophie Hess, who would be his mistress for fifteen years.

He reproaches himself bitterly that he was not with her when she died:

> ". . . My love is with the dead.
> Nor was I there to soothe her latest hour,
> But came to gaze upon a putrid corpse,
> Such as but fools can cherish."

In 1876, when he was forty-three, Nobel—describing himself as "an elderly gentleman"—advertised for a private secretary. Among those who replied was an attractive young woman, the Countess Bertha Kinsky, daughter of an impoverished Austrian family. After an exchange

The proposed new headquarters of the Nobel Center in central Stockholm.

of letters, they met in Paris, and she was given the job. Apparently, Nobel was not as old as he had supposed, and he seems immediately to have lost his heart to the countess. Unfortunately for him her affections were already bestowed. She soon left Nobel to elope with the young Austrian novelist Baron Arthur Gundaccar von Suttner. The two had been secretly engaged, in defiance of her family's wishes. As Bertha von Suttner, she became well known as an ardent worker for peace, and on this subject Nobel carried on a long, and entirely platonic, correspondence with her. After she left her job as secretary, they actually met only twice: the first time not until more than ten years had passed, and the second when she and her husband stayed with Nobel for a few days in Switzerland.

Later that year Nobel was in Austria and made his way to the health resort of Baden-bei-Wien. There, making a casual purchase in a flower shop, he made the acquaintance of an unsophisticated young Jewish girl, Sophie Hess, who was working as an assistant. Nobel became deeply attached to her and eventually set her up in a flat in Paris; marriage was no doubt inappropriate at the time because of their different social status. The difference of religion, too, must have been a factor.

His elder brother Ludwig strongly disapproved of their relationship, and he urged Alfred to break off the liaison. Nevertheless, it persisted for fifteen heartbreaking years. From the beginning, the two were totally unsuited. Alfred was a serious-minded intellectual, twice Sophie's age, preoccupied with international business matters and used to moving in high society. By contrast, Sophie—whom he sometimes referred to as the Troll—was a gay flibbertigibbet of humble origin, utterly resistant to Alfred's attempts to improve her mind and social graces and turn her into a cultivated society woman. She was wildly extravagant (though this was a fault Alfred could endure better than most men), unfaithful, and a general embarrassment. In return, Alfred was patient and, according to his own beliefs, understanding.

A man of different temperament might perhaps have found some compromise, but Alfred was quite out of his depth. Eventually, in 1891, she wrote to say that she had become pregnant by a young Hungarian officer.

Perhaps grateful for the prospect of being relieved of his tempestuous mistress, Alfred replied kindly and settled a handsome annuity on her. Later he even visited her and the child in Vienna.

Despite this, his troubles were not over. When she did eventually marry her officer in 1895, both continued to try to extract more money from him. The persecution even continued after his death in 1896, for Sophie threatened to publish Alfred's letters to her. To avoid scandal, she was bought off by the executors of his will. The liaison was a total disaster, and must have deepened Alfred's melancholy in his later years. History is full of "ifs," but it is interesting to imagine how different his life might have been had he made a happy marriage with an understanding and compatible wife.

TEXT-DEPENDENT QUESTIONS

1. What was Nobel's attitude toward politics?
2. What occurred at the 1892 Peace Conference in Bern, Switzerland?
3. What was Nobel's relationship with Sophie Hess?

RESEARCH PROJECT

The poet Percy Bysshe Shelley, whom Alfred Nobel admired, was a pacifist and supporter of nonviolent resistance to tyranny. Shelley's poem *The Masque of Anarchy* was written in 1819, after the British military attacked British citizens who were demonstrating for political reform, killing six people. Read *The Masque of Anarchy*. What is Shelley describing in the final stanza? Will such a strategy work? Give examples to support your conclusions.

Alfred Nobel's lifelong interest in physics, chemistry, medicine, and literature led him to create the world's most renowned awards.

 # WORDS TO UNDERSTAND

bequest—property or money that is promised to someone in a will.

foreboding—a feeling that something bad will happen.

macabre—something that is gruesome or horrifying.

CHAPTER **6**

The Will and its Consequences

On December 7, 1896, Nobel suffered a stroke, which quickly proved fatal. Ragnar Sohlman, a young Swedish engineer, who had been engaged by Nobel as his personal assistant in 1893, was summoned by telegram from Bofors. However, he did not arrive at San Remo until the evening of December 10, a few hours after Nobel's death. Too late also were two nephews—Hjalmar and Emanuel—who had also been urgently summoned. Nobel's deep **forebodings** had been fulfilled: he died without any "close friend or relation whose kind hand would some day close one's eyes and whisper in one's ear a gentle and sincere word of comfort."

Nobel's old friend, Nathan Söderblom, came from Paris to give a memorial address at a brief ceremony in the house at San Remo. The body was then taken to Stockholm for a formal funeral service in the cathedral, followed by cremation. His ashes were interred in the family grave in the New Cemetery in Stockholm, beside the remains of his parents and of his ill-fated brother, Emil.

Throughout his life Nobel had had a curious obsession that he would be buried alive, and he expressly directed that his veins should be opened before the cremation. Perhaps this obsession was inherited. His father, too, had the same fear, and among the uses he suggested for a kind of chipboard he patented was the following rather **macabre** one: "For coffins, which, while combining cheapness and lightness with tasteful construction and the necessary decoration, could be so made that a person coming to life in them could lift the lid from inside, the lid being provided with airholes for breathing and with a cord attached to a bell."

Alfred Nobel's Will

Meanwhile there had been surprising developments in connection with Nobel's will. On December 15, Sohlman was told that Nobel had made him his executor, jointly with Rudolf Lilljeqvist, a business associate in an electrochemical venture in Sweden. For Sohlman, an inexperienced young engineer still in his twenties, the news was disquieting. No doubt he would have been even more concerned had he known that the task was to involve him in a major international legal dispute conducted in a blaze of publicity. His consolation was that Lilljeqvist was a much more experienced man of business, some fourteen years his senior. For Sohlman this was a curious twist of fate, for the totally unexpected assignment was to affect his entire career.

For the moment, the terms of the will itself were not known, but as soon as the full text had been made available to Sohlman, and he had had some preliminary legal advice, it became clear that its execution presented grave technical difficulties. Nobel's general intentions were clear enough: after certain private **bequests** to members of his family, the residue of his fortune was to be used for the endowment of what we now know as the Nobel Prizes.

The prizes for science were to be awarded by the Swedish Academy of Science; those for medicine by the Caroline Institute in Stockholm; that for literature by the Academy in Stockholm; that for peace by the Norwegian legislature, the Storting. The prizes would be no trifles, for Nobel's estate was valued at 33 million Swedish kroner, an immense sum in those days for a private fortune. (Today, this would be worth about 1.7 billion kroner, or approximately $203 million.)

Although the younger and more inexperienced man, the main burden fell on Sohlman, who had had the most direct personal relationship with

ALFRED NOBEL'S WILL

Albert Nobel's will, drafted and signed by him in Paris in November 1895, distributed funds from his estate to his nephews, nieces, and other family members, former servants, and friends. Once these bequests are outlined, the will reads:

The whole of my remaining realizable estate shall be dealt with in the following way: The capital shall be invested by my executors in safe securities and shall constitute a fund, the interest on which shall be annually distributed in the form of prizes to those who, during the preceding year, shall have conferred the greatest benefit on mankind. The said interest shall be divided into five equal parts, which shall be apportioned as follows: one part to the person who shall have made the most important discovery or invention within the field of physics; one part to the person who shall have made the most important chemical discovery or improvement; one part to the person who shall have made the most important discovery within the domain of physiology or medicine; one part to the person who shall have produced in the field of literature the most outstanding work of an idealistic tendency; and one part to the person who shall have done the most or the best work to promote fraternity between nations, for the abolition or reduction of standing armies and for the holding and promotion of peace congresses. The prizes for physics and chemistry shall be awarded by the Swedish Academy of Sciences; that for physiological or medical work by the Caroline Institute in Stockholm; that for literature by the Academy in Stockholm, and that for champions of peace by a committee of five persons to be elected by the Norwegian Storting. It is my express wish that in awarding the prizes no consideration whatever shall be given to the nationality of the candidates, but that the most worthy shall receive the prize, whether he be a Scandinavian or not.

The Reverend Nathan Söderblom (1866–1931) was the pastor of a Lutheran church that Alfred Nobel attended in Paris. He would later become the archbishop of Uppsala—the head of the Lutheran Church of Sweden—and received the Nobel Prize in 1930.

Nobel; Lilljeqvist had met him only twice. Broadly speaking, his difficulties were of three kinds. Firstly, there were the legal problems. Nobel had written his will in his own hand, in Swedish, apparently without any legal advice whatsoever. It was so imprecise in some respects that the courts might set it aside if it were challenged, as it very soon became clear that it might be. For example, none of the august bodies named by Nobel as adjudicators had been consulted by him. There was no provision for reimbursing them for doing a job that would not only be a labor, however worthwhile, but would involve them in much expense. Furthermore, the mere management of such a large investment was a huge task, and some special body would have to be set up for the purpose. Another legal problem was that of Nobel's domicile: he had homes in Sweden, France, and Italy, and he had in fact spent very little time in Sweden during his lifetime.

A second major difficulty was the question of the "realizable assets" that were to provide funds for the prizes. At the time of his death, Nobel's fortune consisted of large holdings of roughly comparable size in Sweden, Germany, France, Britain, and Russia; there were lesser, but still very considerable, sums in Norway, Austria, and Italy. To liquidate some of these assets could have most unfortunate repercussions, not the least for the surviving members of Nobel's family. For example, Alfred Nobel owned 12 percent share in the Nobel Brothers' Naphtha Company in Russia, which was managed by his nephew Emanuel. The publication of the will prompted rumors of a forced sale, with very adverse effects on the shares of the company. Emanuel Nobel came under heavy pressure from the rest of his family to contest the will.

A further embarrassment to the young Sohlman was a surprisingly violent press campaign against the will, carried on with the tacit approval of certain disappointed members of the family. In all, twenty relatives would have shared the whole estate if the will had been declared invalid. It was scarcely to be wondered at that they were opposed to so large a sum being lost for the benefit of a cause in which they had no personal interest, and which was even attracting public criticism. Generally speaking the campaign was waged at a depressingly insular level. A loyal Swede, it was argued, would not have dissipated his fortune by giving prizes to foreigners. The institutions named by Nobel ought not to take on these additional imposed duties for which, it was said, they were not fit. The delegation of the award for peace to the Norwegian Storting was particularly unpopular, for Sweden's relations with Norway at that time were strained.

Resolving Problems

Considering his youth and inexperience, Sohlman very capably carried out the task thrust upon him. Perhaps his most important single action was to find a first-class legal expert who could advise on matters of which both he and Lilljeqvist were almost wholly ignorant. Their choice was Carl Lindhagen, deputy justice of the Swedish Appeal Court, and events later proved that they could not have done better. Sohlman also established a friendly relationship with the Swedish Consul General in Paris, Gustaf Nordling, who in turn found him a capable French lawyer.

Ragnar Sohlman (1870–1948), Nobel's personal assistant at the time of his death and one of the executors of his will.

All this was achieved by the end of January 1897, within a few weeks of Nobel's death. Speed was vital, for with so large a fortune at stake, it was expected that an attempt would be made to prove that Nobel's home had been France.

The Nobel Peace Center is located near the waterfront in Oslo, Norway.

In that case, all his property in France would have been liable to French tax. If it could be established, however, that his home had been Sweden, then only strictly French securities would be liable for French tax, and the saving would be great. Unfortunately, it seemed that the executors could do nothing about the estate in France until a Swedish court had given them a necessary certificate, and this might take a long time. However, Gustaf Nordling astutely cut this Gordian knot. As a Swedish representative, he provided a certificate to the effect that the executors were acting in accordance with Swedish law and practice.

Lindhagen was summoned to Paris. Thereafter, events moved swiftly and, in some respects, dramatically. First, they made the rounds of a number of

Night view of the Royal Swedish Academy of Science in Stockholm, which hosts the Nobel Museum. Every year the Academy awards the Nobel Prizes in physics, chemistry, and economics.

French banks collecting various securities and documents that Nobel had deposited in them. These were accumulated in a single strong-room in Paris. Meanwhile various members of the Nobel family had arrived, clearly with the intention of getting the will set aside in the French courts. Prudence, if not strict legal ethics, suggested that it would be wise to put the securities beyond the jurisdiction of these courts by sending them to England and Sweden.

A practical difficulty arose because the French postal service would not insure any package for more than 20,000 francs—a mere drop in the ocean in view of the sums involved. The bank of Rothschild, however, was quite used to such transactions, and offered to effect the necessary insurance provided the daily shipment did not exceed 2.5 million francs. Ragnar Sohlman tells how this sum was taken daily for a week from the bank vault to the Swedish Consulate; there the individual items were recorded and packaged before being taken to the Gare du Nord railway station in Paris for dispatch to London. To avoid attracting attention, Sohlman collected the securities himself in a cab—in which he sat with a loaded revolver in his hand in case of attempted robbery. Gustaf Nordling was a great help in all this but found himself getting increasingly embarrassed. On one occasion he was discussing with the relatives the possibility of challenging the will, knowing that in the next room, Sohlman was packing up the securities to put them beyond their reach!

Nordling, therefore, insisted that the relatives be told what had happened. For some reason it was believed that this might be done with the least upset in the course of a lavish dinner party attended by everybody concerned. Perhaps this lessened the shock to the relatives, but it was still considerable. They managed to secure an attachment order to hold what little property remained in France; the major item was Nobel's fine house on the Avenue Malakoff, though the furniture had already been removed and sold. They also sought attachment orders on property in England and Germany, but without success.

Meanwhile, events had been moving in Sweden. Test cases had been brought to see whether the estate came under the jurisdiction of Stockholm or of the County Court of Karlskoga, where the Bofors works were situated. Eventually, the matter was settled in favour of Karlskoga. This led to a decision in France that the courts there had no jurisdiction because at the time of his death, Nobel had been domiciled in Sweden.

Finally, on May 21, 1897, the Swedish government formally instructed its attorney general to have the will declared valid. He was also to give such help as they might desire to the Swedish institutions named by Nobel as adjudicators for the prizes.

Continued Difficulty

Although the tide had turned, there were still many difficulties. The Norwegian Storting had early accepted responsibility for the award of the peace prize, but the Swedish institutions contained members opposed to their taking on the new duties. There was some hope that even if they did so the courts might, as a compromise, decree that the estate should be divided between the relatives and the institutions without putting any special obligations at all on the latter. A minor complication was that Nobel's reference to the "Academy in Stockholm" was too vague, and it could not in law be identified with the Swedish Academy. The Social Democrat Hjalmar Branting bitterly criticized the choice of the Swedish Academy and declared that "it would be better to be rid of both millionaires and donations." (Branting nevertheless accepted the Nobel Peace Prize in 1921.) Although the other institutions finally agreed to cooperate, subject to safeguards, the Academy of Science—after a bitter internal struggle—declined. This created an awkward situation, as was intended. The will could hardly be proved if one of the main adjudicators named in it refused to have anything at all to do with the matter. Such an attitude could only encourage the relatives to renew their efforts to have the will declared null and void.

To resolve the deadlock, it was decided to try again to reach a compromise with the relatives. As a preliminary, a meeting of all the legal advisers—from Sweden, France, Germany, and England—was held in Stockholm in the summer of 1897. All agreed that in none of these countries was any attempt to overturn the will likely to succeed. The position was put to the family, and although they lodged a further protest, the inventory of Nobel's estate was finally submitted to the Karlskoga Court on November 9, 1897, nearly a year after his death. Eventually, estate taxes were agreed upon. It was then possible to begin to dispose of the estate's assets to provide an endowment fund for the prizes.

Meanwhile, some of the disappointed relatives had fallen out among themselves. In December 1897 Emanuel Nobel invited Ragnar Sohlman to spend a few days with him in St. Petersburg for friendly discussion about

ORGANIZATIONS AFFILIATED WITH THE NOBEL PRIZE

The Nobel Prize is affiliated with several organizations and institutions entrusted with different tasks related to the prize. The Nobel Foundation Rights Association was established in 1999 to provide information through a variety of media about the Nobel laureates and their achievements. This non-profit association serves as an umbrella organisation for four other entities:

• Nobel Media, which develops and manages programs, productions, and media rights of the Nobel Prize within the areas of digital and broadcast media;

• The Nobel Museum, housed in the Old Stock Exchange Building (Börshuset) in Stockholm's Old Town, creates interest and spreads knowledge around the natural sciences and culture;

• The Nobel Peace Center, at Rådhusplassen in Oslo, is a showcase that presents information on the history of the Nobel Peace Prize and the work of Peace Prize laureates; and

• The Nobel Prize Education Fund, which supports educational outreach focused on the achievements of Nobel laureates.

the disposal of Nobel's Russian assets, especially his share in the Nobel Brothers' Naphtha Company, whose fortunes were still suffering from the uncertainty. A solution was reached, subject to the agreement of the Swedish branch of the family.

It looked, however, as though this would not be forthcoming, for in February 1898 they started formal legal action to fight the will. It was to

The first Nobel Prize awards ceremony, in 1901.

be a major case, for the defendants were not only the executors but the Swedish government, the Norwegian Storting, and the three adjudicating institutions.

Fortunately, the involvement of the Norwegian Storting caused a delay in the hearing, and in the meantime, better judgment prevailed: a settlement was reached out of court in the summer of 1898. Under its terms, the relatives agreed to accept the general conditions of the will, and forego any claim on the residual estate that was to fund the prizes. In return, they were to receive the interest earned by the assets in 1897, a sizeable sum. It was also agreed that a member of Robert Nobel's family should be consulted when the prize rules were drawn up. A powerful factor was the attitude of

Emanuel Nobel, who had always been a moderating influence. At the very outset, in San Remo, he had reminded young Sohlman that in Russia, the executor of a will is known as *Dushe Prikashshik*—the "spokesman for the soul." For his part he had always wanted to respect his uncle's wishes, so far as the obscurities of the will allowed.

As the legal dust of the family dispute began to settle, the Royal Academy of Sciences announced that it too would join discussions about the award of the prizes. Although many formalities had still to be completed, the agreement in principle of all the parties meant that it was now possible to consider the final objective, the setting up of permanent organizations to comply with Nobel's wishes with regard to the prizes. To make sure that the claims of all candidates were properly examined, and the money properly invested, it was necessary to set up considerable administrative machinery. In the end it was decided to set up a Nobel Foundation of five members, with deputies. The chairman was to be appointed by the Swedish government and the other members by the prize-awarding institutions. Money was set aside for a headquarters, and to cover the expenses of the prize juries.

Not until the turn of the century, however, was all this done. In the summer of 1900, the proposed statutes were approved by the Swedish government. On September 25 of that year, the trustees met for the first time, and Alfred Nobel's intention had at last been achieved. One of the first tasks of the Board of the Foundation was to appoint from their own members an executive director. Appropriately, and almost inevitably, their choice was Ragnar Sohlman, whose determination and single-minded purpose had done so much to bring about the desired end despite all the obstacles.

The first prizes were awarded in Stockholm in 1901. The presentation was made by the Crown Prince of Sweden before a distinguished international gathering, which included Emanuel Nobel and other members of the family. Each prize was worth 150,000 kroner—in those days a very handsome sum indeed, the equivalent of nearly $1 million today. The recipients of the scientific and medical awards were William Conrad

Röntgen of Germany, pioneer of X-rays; Jacobus Henricus van't Hoff of Holland, famous for his work on stereochemistry; and Emil Adolf von Behring of Germany, discoverer of antitoxins and pioneer of their use in the treatment of diphtheria. The prize for literature went to Sully Prudhomme of France, a poet, while the peace prize was shared between Jean Henry Dunant of Switzerland and Frédéric Passy of France.

This glittering ceremony has since been repeated every year, except for the war years, and over 900 of the world's most intellectually gifted men and women have benefited from Nobel's generosity. Today, each prize is worth 9 million kroner (a little more than $1 million in 2018 dollars) but, especially in science and medicine, prizes are commonly shared between two or three laureates. To a great extent, this reflects the fact that in these fields, progress depends more on brilliant teamwork than on individual genius, a development that might not have had Nobel's approval. The dignified formality of the proceedings makes it hard to remember that they arose from controversy and strife. Perhaps it is appropriate that this should have been so. As Nobel was a controversial figure in his lifetime, so he remained controversial in the fulfillment of his wishes after his death.

TEXT-DEPENDENT QUESTIONS

1. Who were the executors of Alfred Nobel's will?
2. What is the Norwegian Storting?
3. When did the Swedish government approve the statutes that established the Nobel Prizes?
4. Who was the first director of the board of the Nobel Foundation?

 RESEARCH PROJECT

Go to the website www.nobelprize.org to find a list of all Nobel Prize laureates since 1901. Choose one laureate from the list. Using the internet or your school library, find out more about that person's life and career. Write a short two-page biography that provides information about the person's work and accomplishments that were deemed worthy of a Nobel Prize.

Chronology

c. 500 BCE
Inflammable materials begin to be used in military engagements.

c. 7th century CE
"Greek Fire" is used by the Byzantines.

c. 11th century
Chinese discover the inflammable qualities of saltpeter.

1346
Roger Bacon describes gunpowder. The Battle of Crécy is the first major European battle in which gunpowder is used.

1376
Explosive shells are probably used by Venetians at Battle of Jadra.

1618–48
Thirty Years' War; rifles used extensively for first time.

1761
Birth of Henry Shrapnel, inventor of the shrapnel shell.

1799
Birth of C. F. Schönbein, discoverer of guncotton.

1803
Introduction of percussion cap. Shrapnel shells officially approved for use by British Army.

1807
Birth of T. J. Pelouze, distinguished French chemist under whom Nobel worked briefly.

1812
Birth of Ascanio Sobrero, discoverer of nitroglycerin.

1827
Birth of Sir Frederick Abel, British explosives expert.

1833
Birth of Alfred Nobel.

1842
Immanuel Nobel and his family move to Moscow.

1845
Discovery of guncotton.

1846
Guncotton patented in England.

1847
Discovery of the explosive, nitroglycerin. An explosion at a guncotton factory in Kent, England, kills twenty-one people.

c. 1850–52
Alfred Nobel visits the United States

1854–56
Crimean War; Immanuel Nobel's mines used by Russian forces.

1863
Immanuel Nobel begins manufacturing new form of gunpowder.

1863
Nitroglycerin factory established by Immanuel and Alfred Nobel.

1864
Death of Emil Nobel in explosion at the Nobel nitroglycerin factory.

1865
First high-explosives factory established near Stockholm. Nobel's first factory outside Sweden is established at Krümmel, near Hamburg. J. F. Schulze discovers smokeless gunpowder.

1866
Krümmel factory destroyed in explosion.

1867
Dynamite patented.

1868
The Giant Powder Co. in San Francisco is the first American venture in high explosives.

1869
An Act of Parliament is passed to restrict use of nitroglycerin or preparations containing it in Britain.

1872
Death of Immanuel Nobel, Alfred's father.

1875
Alfred Nobel addresses Society of Arts, London.

1875
Blasting gelatin perfected.

1877
The Nobel Brothers' Naphtha Co. formed in Russia.

1888
Nobel introduces ballistite.

1891
Nobel leaves France to live in Italy.

1892
Berne Peace Congress impresses Nobel.

1893–95
High Court case in Britain over infringement of the ballistite/cordite patent.

1893
Nobel decides to leave part of fortune as prize for promotion of world peace.

1896
Death of Alfred Nobel.

1897
Nobel's will declared valid by the Swedish courts.

1900
Board of Nobel Foundation formed under Nobel's will for administration of the prizes.

1901
First Nobel Prizes awarded.

Further Reading

Akhavan, Jacqueline. *The Chemistry of Explosives.* London: Royal Society of Chemistry, 2011.

Binns, Tristan Boyer. *Alfred Nobel: Innovative Thinker.* Chicago: Franklin Watts, 2004.

Fant, Kenne. *Alfred Nobel: A Biography.* Trans. by Marianne Ruuth. New York: Arcade Publishing, 2014.

Kelly, Jack. *Gunpowder: Alchemy, Bombards, and Pyrotechnics: The History of the Explosive that Changed the World.* New York: Basic Books, 2014.

Norrby, Erling. *Nobel Prizes and Notable Discoveries.* Hackensack, NJ: World Scientific, 2016.

Wargin, Kathy-Jo. *Alfred Nobel: The Man Behind the Peace Prize.* Illus. by Zachary Pullen. Ann Arbor, Mich.: Sleeping Bear Press, 2009.

Worek, Michael. *The Nobel Prize: The Story of Alfred Nobel and the Most Famous Prize in the World.* San Francisco: Firefly Books, 2010.

Internet Resources

https://www.nobelprize.org

The official website of the Nobel Prize includes information on Alfred Nobel, as well as news about the annual awards and short biographies of prizewinners.

http://www.bbc.co.uk/history/historic_figures/nobel_alfred.shtml

The British Broadcasting Company (BBC) provides a short biography of Alfred Nobel at this site.

http://www.pbs.org/wgbh/nova

The website of NOVA, a science series that airs on PBS. The series produces in-depth science programming on a variety of topics, from the latest breakthroughs in technology to the deepest mysteries of the natural world.

http://www.biology4kids.com/files/studies_scimethod.html

A simple explanation of the scientific method is available at this website for young people.

http://www.livescience.com

The website Live Science is regularly updated with articles on scientific topics and new developments or discoveries.

Publisher's Note: The websites listed on this page were active at the time of publication. The publisher is not responsible for websites that have changed their address or discontinued operation since the date of publication. The publisher reviews and updates the websites each time the book is reprinted.

Series Glossary of Key Terms

anomaly—something that differs from the expectations generated by an established scientific idea. Anomalous observations may inspire scientists to reconsider, modify, or come up with alternatives to an accepted theory or hypothesis.

evidence—test results and/or observations that may either help support or help refute a scientific idea. In general, raw data are considered evidence only once they have been interpreted in a way that reflects on the accuracy of a scientific idea.

experiment—a scientific test that involves manipulating some factor or factors in a system in order to see how those changes affect the outcome or behavior of the system.

hypothesis—a proposed explanation for a fairly narrow set of phenomena, usually based on prior experience, scientific background knowledge, preliminary observations, and logic.

natural world—all the components of the physical universe, as well as the natural forces at work on those things.

objective—to consider and represent facts without being influenced by biases, opinions, or emotions. Scientists strive to be objective, not subjective, in their reasoning about scientific issues.

observe—to note, record, or attend to a result, occurrence, or phenomenon.

science—knowledge of the natural world, as well as the process through which that knowledge is built through testing ideas with evidence gathered from the natural world.

subjective—referring to something that is influenced by biases, opinions, and/or emotions. Scientists strive to be objective, not subjective, in their reasoning about scientific issues.

test—an observation or experiment that could provide evidence regarding the accuracy of a scientific idea. Testing involves figuring out what one would expect to observe if an idea were correct and comparing that expectation to what one actually observes.

theory—a broad, natural explanation for a wide range of phenomena in science. Theories are concise, coherent, systematic, predictive, and broadly applicable, often integrating and generalizing many hypotheses. Theories accepted by the scientific community are generally strongly supported by many different lines of evidence. However, theories may be modified or overturned as new evidence is discovered.

Index

About the Author

Timmy Warner is a 2009 graduate of the University of West Virginia, where he studied creative writing and English literature. He currently works in New York. This is his first book.

Photo Credits

Everett Collection: 44, 46 (bottom), 48, 50, 56; IMSL: 23; Library of Congress: 25, 29, 32, 52, 59; Nobel Center: 64; image provided by the Nobel Foundation: 1, 6, 21, 34, 47, 68, 73, 74, 80; Office of Coast Survey/National Ocean Service/NOAA: 15; used under license from Shutterstock, Inc.: 36, 42 55, 63, 76; Miroslav Kresac / Shutterstock.com: 13; Lestertair / Shutterstock.com: 11; Miroslav110 / Shutterstock.com: 75; SvetlanaSF / Shutterstock.com: 18; Thor Jorgen Udvang / Shutterstock.com: 92; United Nations photo: 8; Wellcome Library: 12, 20, 24, 40; Wikimedia Commons: 26, 38, 49, 72.